VAN CARLTON DETECTIVE AGENCY

Van Carlton Detective Agency: The Burgundy Diamond
Author: Kambiz Mostofizadeh
Publisher: Mikazuki Publishing House
ISBN-13: 978-0-9910285-0-4

PRINTED IN THE UNITED STATES OF AMERICA

EDUCATION IS THE KEY TO HAPPINESS

www.MikazukiPublishingHouse.com

VAN CARLTON DETECTIVE AGENCY

TABLE OF CONTENTS

VAN CARLTON DETECTIVE AGENCY

CHAPTER ONE

THE AGENCY

Steve Van Carlton was not your average business owner. Two tours in Iraq made him tough as nails, but Steve had a soft side to him. Today was his girlfriend's birthday and he was getting ready to go to work. The phone rang. It was his secretary reminding him of his appointment at 10am. Steve was the owner of the Van Carlton Agency on Sunset Boulevard. He had 5 detectives working in his office and he was partnered with agencies in New York, London, Amsterdam, and Dubai. He was a man of culture too as he had box seat tickets to

VAN CARLTON DETECTIVE AGENCY

an opera tucked away in his two buttoned 150

thread blazer. Steve entered the garage in and

sat in his bulletproof BMX 740il, turned on the

motor, adjusted his rearview mirror, opened the

garage door, and pulled out. Steve left his

million dollar house on Mount Olympus, a

fashionable and luxurious guard gated

community of mansions in the hills of Los

Angeles, slowly driving down the winding road

that met with Sepulveda Blvd. It took him 15

minutes to pull in to the parking garage of his

Sunset office building in that the Van Carlton

Agency was located. He parked, walked to the

elevator, finally arriving at the 10th floor. As the

VAN CARLTON DETECTIVE AGENCY

elevator door opened, his personal assistant Marin shoved papers on a clipboard in to his hands for his approval and signature.

"I just got here!" said Van Carlton

Marin replied "It's our busiest week boss, we just took on 3 new clients, and the Diamond exhibition is in town…."

"Oh yes! The International Royal Jewel exhibit, we have been contracted to protect the Burgundy Diamond among other items there. Call our logistics coordinator and have him send a detailed list of exhibitors." said Van Carlton

VAN CARLTON
DETECTIVE AGENCY

Marin responded "Right away boss" and walked in to a room adjacent to Van Carlton's main office.

CHAPTER TWO

THE EMAIL

Van Carlton sat behind his desk, flipping on the 30 inch LCD monitor across from him, and starting browsing emails on his desktop computer. Van Carlton was constantly getting offers to take important cases and in many ways fashioned himself as a modern Sherlock Holmes, always solving the crime and capturing the bad guys. But a long time had passed since the innocence of his childhood.

VAN CARLTON DETECTIVE AGENCY

Van Carlton was not dreaming anymore and he had become both rich and well known because of the cases he had solved for wealthy industrialists. Occasionally he would even receive a phone call from a fast talking, sharp witted talent agent offering to make a movie about his exploits. Van Carlton would laugh about it and tell them he was much less important than these producers imagined. Either way, success had found him but he built the hope of his future success on the cases he could solve today. One email in particular struck him as being very interesting. Van Carlton opened the email and to his surprise it

VAN CARLTON DETECTIVE AGENCY

was not an offer to solve a crime. The email's content was an anonymous tip giving information about a crime that had not yet materialized.

The email read:

The Burgundy Diamond will be stolen and there is nothing you or anyone can do about it.

The Fox

Van Carlton thought for a moment, going over the possibles or the individuals that could have sent this email. He then decided it wasn't worth the time and made preparations

VAN CARLTON DETECTIVE AGENCY

to leave for the International Royal Diamond

Exhibition. He arrived in front of the Biltmore

Hotel, observed the attendees exiting their

rented limousines, and then he entered the

lobby. The Biltmore Hotel was a landmark in

Los Angeles and Van Carlton was no stranger

to it. Van Carlton's high school prom was held

there and he was reminiscing of his mis-spent

youth. He walked in to the gift shop, his

favorite store in any hotel and purchased

chewing gum. As he walked up the stairs

leading to the entrance of the hall hosting the

Royal Diamond Exhibition, Van Carlton spotted

an old friend of his. It was Jennifer Parson, his

VAN CARLTON
DETECTIVE AGENCY

high school girlfriend, but their relationship had never really finished. Jennifer would see Van Carlton whenever it was convenient and Van Carlton was flexible enough to know that if he pressured her, he might lose her entirely. So on and on it went and here she was again.

"I see you have a thing for diamonds..." said Van Carlton

"What gal doesn't?" she replied

"Excellent point" said Van Carlton

Jennifer walked closer and hugged him.

"It is so great to see you." she said.

VAN CARLTON DETECTIVE AGENCY

"I was going to say the same thing except I would never say it surrounded by diamonds." Replied Van Carlton

Jennifer said "You always were afraid of commitment."

"Well….would you commit to accommodating me to tonight as my date" he said

"I thought you would never ask…" she said.

They walked in arms locked in to each other like an old couple and starting walking through the maze of stands holding jewels from India, Iran, England, Thailand, and countries no one had heard of. People were drinking and talking

VAN CARLTON DETECTIVE AGENCY

with one another, some passing business cards and some exchanging social networking information. The Mayor of Los Angeles was in attendance as he was a large fan of anywhere the press would be and tonight in Los Angeles, this is where the sharks were feeding.

The largest amount of people were gathered around one stand in particular, a large cylindrical glass case mounted on a marble square slab. There was one security guard standing one meter from the stand and there were numerous security guards roaming throughout the exhibition hall. Van Carlton remembered the note forecasting of the theft of

VAN CARLTON
DETECTIVE AGENCY

the Burgundy Diamond. He looked around

observing the well to do guests that were

attending this event. The Ladies in attendance

were dripping in diamond necklaces and

earrings, dressed in expensive Stefano and

Ungaro dresses with the latest designer Gucci

handbags. Men were wearing tuxedos or ties

with top hats or fedoras. Who could be the

thief among these people? Van Carlton

decided to walk among the people a bit and

make small observations. If I was a thief, how

would I be acting, he thought to himself.

Would it be nervous behavior that would give

away the thief or just the demeanor? What if

VAN CARLTON DETECTIVE AGENCY

the thief is not even here is what Van Carlton

thought and greater reflection validated his

belief. A tall fellow approached Van Carlton,

gave him a business card and started a

conversation with him. Van Carlton looked at

the business card he was clutching with both

hands.

The Business Card said:

Mark Jostler
TechGlobus Capital
424-XXX-XXXX

Jostler said "I want to make you an offer

Mr.Van Carlton"

VAN CARLTON DETECTIVE AGENCY

"I am listening" responded Van Carlton

CHAPTER THREE

THE MEETING

"Please follow me Mr. Van Carlton, I am hoping you can appreciate the need for privacy."

Van Carlton hesitated for a moment, then followed Jostler to a private suite with two burly security guards protecting the entrance. The door opened and Van Carlton entered, noticing a group of older gentlemen sitting around a table adorned with flowers. A distinguished gentlemen and scholar known by his nom de

VAN CARLTON DETECTIVE AGENCY

plume Morris Lavarian for his writings on history, greeted Van Carlton.

"Welcome to our table Mr. Van Carlton. Please have a seat. You may be wondering why we summoned you to this private meeting. We wanted to announce that we have sold the Burgundy Diamond to Mr. Jostler. Yesterday we received a note that alarmed us. We wanted to share it with you, so we have summoned you here today. Allow me to read you the contents of the note."

Van Carlton interrupted Lavarian and said "Allow me gentlemen as I have received a

VAN CARLTON
DETECTIVE AGENCY

similar note. Let me guess, your note says something to the effect of the Burgundy Diamond will be stolen and there is nothing that you or anyone can do about it. Am I right gentlemen?"

The men sitting at the table began murmuring among themselves, some shocked, some surprised looking at one another.

Van Carlton continued "If he is here we will find him but I assure you gentlemen that no thief could steal such an item in a room filled with people. The Burgundy Diamond is held in a glass case with one security guard standing a

VAN CARLTON
DETECTIVE AGENCY

whispers throw away from it. I assure you gentlemen the treasure is safe." Van Carlton smiled.

"Even so we doubt the same will hold true when the room is emptied. We would like you to watch the Burgundy Diamond over the next few days....." said Lavarian

"Rest assured gentlemen, that is why you have hired me. This is a simple game of cat and mouse. If the crime happens, I will catch him. Now if you will excuse me, I have an exhibition to attend. Is that all gentlemen?" responded Van Carlton

VAN CARLTON DETECTIVE AGENCY

The men sitting around the table nodded to each other and rose as Van Carlton walked out of the room. Van Carlton wasn't taking any chances. He walked back in to the hall still filled with exhibition attendees in their finest furs. Van Carlton re-approached the Burgundy Diamond. Everything seemed normal and the security guard standing next to it was as vigilant as possible. No need to stick around anymore Van Carlton thought, so he decided to find Jennifer Parson among the crowd. The balcony was the first thought that came to him as he knew Jennifer's dislike for large crowds and crowded scenes. Van Carlton walked out on to the balcony and sure enough, she was there nursing her wine glass and staring at the landscape of the city. Jennifer loved city views and the city lights, a memory she cherished from the times Van Carlton and her would drive up Topanga Canyon, park at Lovers Lane, staring out at the eccentric metropolis she called home.

"I never thought you would show up. I thought I had lost you again." said Jennifer

Van Carlton responded "You could never lose me darling. Business was keeping me busy."

VAN CARLTON DETECTIVE AGENCY

"Sure. It is always the business. Time for the business. Time for the criminal. Where is the time for your love." said Jennifer

Van Carlton responded "I am here now darling. I won't leave you again tonight...."

"It is getting close to my bedtime. Plus you know how I get at midnight; I want to turn in to a pumpkin. I think we should be leaving now." said Jennifer

They walked through the hall drawing the attentions of onlookers as they walked down the stairs exiting the gaze of rumor-mongers and paparazzi. Jennifer Parson and Steve Van

VAN CARLTON DETECTIVE AGENCY

Carlton entered a white limousine and began their trip to Jennifer's Malibu villa, facing the warm glowing Pacific Ocean. The night was still young.....

Van Carlton was in a sort of inebriated dream like state. The thoughts of his years spent with Jennifer were racing through his mind. The exotic trips they took to destinations like Thailand and gambling in Macao, eating breakfast in London and dinner in Berlin. They had travelled extensively together and were not only comfortable being together, they shared common interests. When they were younger, in their early teens, they loved spending holidays

VAN CARLTON DETECTIVE AGENCY

together and hiking up the snowed capped

mountains of Southern California. They both

loved hiking, the mountain air, and camping in

destinations like Yosemite and the Los Padres

National Forest.

The next morning Jennifer turned in bed,

placing her left arm around Van Carlton's non-

existent body. Van Carlton was not there, she

sat up in her bed and looked out of her window

towards the beach.

A muscular figure emerged from the water,

walking from the ocean on to the beach

VAN CARLTON DETECTIVE AGENCY

towards the villa. Jennifer walked out on to the balcony in a bikini overlooking the ocean.

"Great day for a swim." Jennifer said

Jennifer threw Van Carlton a towel, which Van Carlton started drying his body with.

"Why don't you join me?" Van Carlton responded

Jennifer thought about it, but was too busy admiring the muscles and curvature of Van Carlton's tone body.

VAN CARLTON DETECTIVE AGENCY

CHAPTER FOUR

JENNIFER

"I am enjoying the view." Jennifer said

Van Carlton smiled and walked on to the balcony, standing shoulder to shoulder with Jennifer looking out on to the beach and the bluish-green beauty of the Pacific Ocean. Van Carlton threw his left arm around Jennifer and kissed her right cheek.

"What do you have planned for today?" Van Carlton said

"It's Saturday." Jennifer responded

"And?" Van Carlton said

VAN CARLTON DETECTIVE AGENCY

"And I thought it might be nice if you could take me out to a nice place and take me shopping for a change." Jennifer said

"Let me get dressed darling." Van Carlton said as he walked inside the house.

Van Carlton and Jennifer zipped through the windy Topanga Canyon road and slowly pulled in to the gravel driveway of his favorite restaurant, Inn at the Seventh Ray. This was a trendy but unpretentious restaurant, regularly visited by celebrities, nestled in the hills of Topanga Canyon between Malibu and the San Fernando Valley. Jennifer and Van Carlton

VAN CARLTON
DETECTIVE AGENCY

exited the bulletproof BMX 740il and walked in to the restaurant, towards the back where Van Carlton's assistant had reserved a table from the night before.

"Oooh, it's Fabio, my first celebrity sighting of the day." Jennifer said

"I thought I was your celebrity." Van Carlton responded

"You are my celebrity." Jennifer said

"Good to know" Van Carlton said

VAN CARLTON
DETECTIVE AGENCY

They sat down and their server walked in. Their waiter took their order and Jennifer started making light conversation.

"Wouldn't this place be great for a wedding?" Jennifer said

Van Carlton looked around the restaurant he had hosted meetings and events so many times in the past. The seating areas consisted of wooden decks with ornate table decorations. It seemed as if the hill adjacent to the restaurant and the seating areas were converging in one natural atmosphere. There was a creek flowing on one side of the

VAN CARLTON DETECTIVE AGENCY

restaurant with wild flowers growing between the seating areas. Van Carlton felt at peace at that moment, a feeling he had not been able to feel for quite some time. He felt as if though he was being rejuvenated by the combination of sun, sitting with his teenage sweetheart, and the nature setting. Their waitress served their food and they began eating.

"You never answered my question" Jennifer said

Van Carlton responded "I thought it was a rhetorical question."

"Never mind" Jennifer said

VAN CARLTON DETECTIVE AGENCY

Van Carlton responded "Don't be cross darling, when our time comes, it will just happen. Don't you believe in destiny?"

"Just eat your food" Jennifer said

After dessert, they got in the 740il and head to the newly mass renovated Topanga Mall. Van Carlton grew up in Woodland Hills and had fond memories of that area. Playing baseball in Shoup Park, hiking up Knapp Park, attending Taft High School and Pierce College, and walking on Ventura Blvd to take the ill-dreaded Los Angeles Rapid Transit District buses to get around. The young handsome Van Carlton

VAN CARLTON DETECTIVE AGENCY

spent many hours as a teenager walking though the mall meeting girls, to exchange phone numbers with. But the teenage Van Carlton was a bit wild back then, as he was a DJ and a drummer. He was always fond of meeting new women and he did Tae Kwan Do 4 days a week to maintain his health and good looks.

They parked and walked to the massive entrance of the Topanga Mall, entering in to a department store that Van Carlton had briefly worked at, at the time of the 1994 Northridge earthquake. They briskly moved through the crowded aisles filled with shoppers, perfume sprayers, and seasonal staff, finally entering the main area of the mall. They stopped at the first store that sparked Jennifer's interest, the women's shoe store. Of course, Van Carlton thought to himself. Jennifer completed her purchases and walked out but Van Carlton grabbed her bags and carried them for her.

"Can you ask for a better assistant?" Van Carlton said

Jennifer responded "For today? No"

Van Carlton responded "So what's next?"

"I need a new bikini." she said

VAN CARLTON DETECTIVE AGENCY

Van Carlton responded "Who am I to say no. After you, I'll follow."

Jennifer walked in to Victoria's Secret, a trendy women's shop for undergarments, lingerie, and beachwear. Van Carlton always liked walking in to a Victoria's Secret shop because he was able to attract smiles from women that saw him as the only man in their store. But the truth was that Van Carlton was a rebel at heart and he disliked how the major brands had swallowed up the unique brands that had been icons in Los Angeles. To Van Carlton, Victoria's Secret was a copy of Frederick's of Hollywood, but not just a copy it took a unique

VAN CARLTON
DETECTIVE AGENCY

brand and made a McDonald's style franchise of it. But women know what they like and Van Carlton wanted to keep Jennifer both interested and happy, so he made himself flexible to her requests. She completed her purchases and walked out, Van Carlton again grabbing her bags.

"Did you get what you want" Van Carlton said

Jennifer responded "I always get what I want"

"Good. If we are done shopping, want to see a movie? Van Carlton said

"Love to. You pick." Jennifer said

VAN CARLTON DETECTIVE AGENCY

They walked over to the multiplex adjacent to the mall and purchased two tickets for the newest action movie. Van Carlton purchased the standard package he gets every time he goes to the movies, a medium popcorn lightly buttered, large pack of Twizzlers, and a large Diet Coke with two straws. Jennifer and Van Carlton took their seats and the movie began. It was a two hour session of violence, sex, drug use, and criminality, unfortunately the current formula for successful movie production which has become so cliché. For Van Carlton, he was not interested in the movie as it reminded him too much of the reality that shapes the

VAN CARLTON DETECTIVE AGENCY

criminal underworld in any major metropolis, rather he was giving all his attention to Jennifer. The movie was really an excuse to spend time with her.

The movie ended and they exited the door at the lowest point of the theater, entering the parking lot and being showered by light from the hot Los Angeles sun.

"Well that was enjoyable. I had a great time." Van Carlton said

"Me too. Thank you." Jennifer said with a smile

"Canter's?" Van Carlton said

VAN CARLTON DETECTIVE AGENCY

Jennifer responded "Canter's"

Canter's was an old haunt of Van Carlton's, he spent many hours studying there when he was attending USC. Canter's was opened in the early 1900's by Jewish immigrants and served the best Pastrami west of the Mississippi River. Jennifer and Van Carlton pulled in to the parking lot of Fairfax Blvd and parked. They walked in to Canter's which first opens to a bakery with the most delightful smells from the cookies and pastries filling the lobby. The host sat them at his favorite table, above them the original hand painted art deco themed glass ceiling from the early 1900's when it was a

VAN CARLTON
DETECTIVE AGENCY

theater. The waitress approached them and Van Carlton ordered for the both of them, two pastramis on rye bread with two strawberry lemonades. Their food was served 15 minutes later and they ate while conversing.

"So how did the meeting go?" Jennifer said

Van Carlton responded "Meeting? What meeting? You were following me?"

"I came back from the bar and I saw you leave so I followed you. I saw you walk in to a room and the door shut so I went to the balcony and waited." Jennifer said

VAN CARLTON DETECTIVE AGENCY

Van Carlton responded "Oh that meeting. It went….well. New clients. We shall see. I don't take on all clients, but this is a special case. What about you? What are you doing these days? Still teaching women how to beat up their husbands?"

"Ha. Ha. Very funny mister whodunit. I teach self-defense. You better watch it or I may have to give you a live demonstration right here." Jennifer said

Van Carlton responded "Okay, settle down sweetheart. I submit."

VAN CARLTON DETECTIVE AGENCY

"You better" Jennifer said and punched Van Carlton in his upper arm.

Van Carlton settled the bill and they left driving on Sunset Boulevard towards Hollywood. The tourists were combing the streets for the next celebrity, mascots and impersonators filled the sidewalk, and street hawkers were peddling their wares. The sun was starting to go down and the bars and clubs were opening their doors for the night to welcome their first customers. Van Carlton decided to stop at the Saddle Back Ranch restaurant for a drink and to make a few calls. Van Carlton pulled in to the parking lot and the valet parkers opened

VAN CARLTON DETECTIVE AGENCY

the car doors as Jennifer and he exited. The

Saddle Back Ranch was quickly becoming a

Sunset Boulevard icon as many important

events were held there as well as being a

vibrant bar for young socialites. The all wooden

construction design gave it a warm atmosphere

and it featured a mechanical riding bull in the

middle of its hall. Van Carlton had briefly

dabbled in politics, supporting John McCain's

presidential bid in 2000, and had attended the

Saddle Back Ranch for that event. They

walked up the stairs to the 2nd floor overlooking

Sunset and Van Carlton received a call from

this personal assistant Marin.

VAN CARLTON DETECTIVE AGENCY

CHAPTER FIVE

THE OWNER

"Marin, what do you have for me?"

Marin responded "I have bad news boss. The Burgundy Diamond was stolen."

"What?? When?" Van Carlton said

Marin responded "Last night. Apparently the thieves did it after the exhibition. I have a message for you from a Mr. Jostler of TechGlobus Capital."

"What time was the message?" Van Carlton said

VAN CARLTON DETECTIVE AGENCY

Marin responded "5pm today"

"What time was the burglary?" Van Carlton said

Marin responded "3am-5am. The time has not been accurately decided. You have been requested to visit the crime scene."

"Requested? Requested by whom?" Van Carlton said

Marin said "Mr. Jostler. He is claiming that he is the rightful owner of the Burgundy Diamond. He claims to have brought it to the exhibition with a Mr. Lavarian."

VAN CARLTON
DETECTIVE AGENCY

"Okay, I am heading there now. Text me a list of attendees from the exhibition. I will try to see if I can take a look at their video surveillance. Also call our Forensics specialist, I want him in our office tonight. I think we will need him." Van Carlton said

Van Carlton ended the call and told Jennifer of the situation, so they left to the Biltmore Hotel. They arrived in front of the hotel and walked in, an aide to Mr. Lavarian greeted them and took them through the lines of police officers and yellow tape guarding the scene of the crime and all the clues it held. There was the glass case on the marble square slab but no sight of

VAN CARLTON
DETECTIVE AGENCY

the Burgundy Diamond. Van Carlton

approached the glass case with Jennifer

trailing behind him. He opened up a black bag

that contained an array of digital-analog

devices for investigation. Manually dusting and

fingerprinting were a thing of the past. One of

his devices, the CrimeLife Scanner could

digitally scan a fingerprint not seeable to the

human eye and then simultaneously search

over 50 international crime databases for a

match. Van Carlton took out the CrimeLife

Scanner and followed the curvature of the

glass from the bottom of it to its top. Each time

the CrimeLife Scanner picked up a partial

VAN CARLTON DETECTIVE AGENCY

fingerprint, it gave a faint single sound that was more akin to a blip from a radar screen. Each time it found it found a whole fingerprint, the CrimeLife Scanner would sound off three times loudly. In the end, over 1000 fingerprints were found, but the CrimeLife Scanner only found three individuals that had a 90% or greater match. All three lived in Los Angeles and all three were wealthy industrialists.

Their names were:

John Kilroy, Real Estate Mogul

Rory Poplov, Construction Developer

Amory Nardin, Software Developer

VAN CARLTON
DETECTIVE AGENCY

All of these men had ties to criminal funding

and criminal organizations in the past, despite

never having been convicted successfully of

committing a crime. They all operated among

the gray areas of society, where ethics

disappears and rugged capitalism becomes the

modus operandi. Van Carlton walked to the

elevator and entered with Jennifer aside him.

Van Carlton pressed the L button for Lobby

and as the elevator started moving, he pressed

the alarm button. A voice from the intercom

speaker rang back.

"How can I help you gentlemen?" the security

guard said

VAN CARLTON DETECTIVE AGENCY

Van Carlton responded "What floor are you located on?"

"The Lobby floor, security room behind the elevator" the security guard said

The elevator arrived at the Lobby floor, Jennifer and Van Carlton exited and walked around the exterior of the elevator shaft to the security room and knocked.

The security guard opened the door.

"How can I help you gentlemen?" said the security guard

VAN CARLTON DETECTIVE AGENCY

"I am Steve Van Carlton from the Van Carlton Detective Agency. I have been hired to investigate the theft of the Burgundy Diamond. Can you help me? I want to see surveillance tapes...."

The security guard responded "I would have to speak with my Manager. Do you have a warrant? I can be fired from my work. "

"I am not police. I am a private investigator. Nobody wants you to lose your job, we just want to see footage from 3am to 5am. Can you help me?" Van Carlton said

VAN CARLTON DETECTIVE AGENCY

Jennifer waited outside while Van Carlton entered the security room. The security guard played back the footage. It was white noise. The disc had been erased and more than likely replaced.

"'It's blank" the security guard said

"Thank you officer, you have been more than helpful. I think we are done here. Let's go my darling. " Van Carlton said

Van Carlton let Jennifer know that the information sought had not been collected and that they should head back to the Van Carlton Agency for further investigation of matters.

VAN CARLTON DETECTIVE AGENCY

They arrived at the Van Carlton Agency and Marin ran towards them.

Marin said "I found the list of attendees but I could not text it to you in time so I went ahead and printed a cross-referenced list of attendees that have any association with criminals. The names are...."

Van Carlton was excited to review this list as these would be the leads that he would follow up to find the Burgundy Diamond. The investigation begins, Van Carlton thought.

VAN CARLTON DETECTIVE AGENCY

CHAPTER SIX

UNUSUAL SUSPECTS

"Wait, let me guess….Nardin, Poplov, Kilroy. The CrimeLife Scanner came up with the same information. Good to know we are on the same page. " Van Carlton said

With files in hand, he headed to his all-in-one copy machine and made copies of the files.

"Marin bring me a cup of coffee please" Van Carlton said

Van Carlton sat on the leather couch in his office and Marin brought him his guilty pleasure, a cup of caffeinated coffee with

VAN CARLTON DETECTIVE AGENCY

cream. Jennifer was sitting behind Van

Carlton's desk cruising through her favorite

social networks, posting about her weekly self-

defense classes that had become so popular

recently. Van Carlton decided to follow up on

his first lead, the software developer Nardin.

This short and ugly software developer had

made his money by betraying his business

partners and stealing business ideas, but the

gray areas that rugged capitalists operate

under were neither legit nor illegitimate.

Nardin's had an office in Westwood, an area in

Los Angeles popular to UCLA students and

well-to-do Iranian-American immigrants. Van

VAN CARLTON DETECTIVE AGENCY

Carlton and Jennifer left for Nardin's office and entered its parking lot. The office was a run-of-the-mill office building built in the 1970's with stucco ceilings and carpeted floors. Van Carlton would have expected the Los Angeles office of Nardin to be exquisitely designed but Nardin was famous for being miserly. The secretary greeted Van Carlton and Jennifer and lead them to a waiting room until Nardin arrived.

"How can I help you?" Nardin said as he opened the door leading to the waiting room

VAN CARLTON DETECTIVE AGENCY

Van Carlton responded "Hello Mr. Nardin. My name is Steve Van Carlton from Van Carlton Detective Agency and I have been contracted to investigate the theft of the Burgundy Diamond."

"Do you have a warrant?" Nardin said

"We are not police. We are here to ask you a few questions. Can you help us?" Van Carlton responded

"I don't see how I can. How does the theft of jewels in an exhibition involve me Mr. Van Carlton? " said Nardin

VAN CARLTON DETECTIVE AGENCY

"Your fingerprints were found on the glass case that held the Burgundy Diamond. Can you see how this involves you? Would you like to tell us why your fingerprint could have been found on the glass case that held the diamond?" said Van Carlton

Nardin responded "I visited the exhibition yesterday as did thousands of others. I was not the only person at the exhibition, in fact they sold tickets and advertised the event. You were also at the event, were you not?"

"I was at the event but my fingerprint was not on the glass. Yours was and you have had ties

VAN CARLTON DETECTIVE AGENCY

with certain individuals that have links with organized crime." Van Carlton said

"Ties with certain individuals? What are you implying? Look, if you want information, of which I have none, you are approaching me in a rather rude manner. I resent your hardball police interrogation tactics. This talk is over." Nardin said

Nardin pressed a button on his phone and the door to his office opened, two security guards entered and put their hands on Jennifer and Van Carlton.

VAN CARLTON DETECTIVE AGENCY

One of the security guards said "You all are going to have to leave. Meeting is over."

Van Carlton and Jennifer stood up and walked to the door leading to the outside hallway and Nardin trailed after them.

"Talk to you soon Nardin" Van Carlton said

"I am sure of it." Nardin said

As they walked to the parking lot, Van Carlton began to review the meeting he just had. Was Nardin hiding something, someone that had enriched his pocket by betrayal and distrust surely could not be one hundred percent honest when questioned. This was to be

VAN CARLTON
DETECTIVE AGENCY

expected, Van Carlton thought. Van Carlton

and Jennifer got in to the car and headed to

speak with the next person on his list. They

arrived at the guard gated Bel-Air community of

mini and mega-mansions. The security guard

waved them through and they arrived in front of

the Poplov residence. Poplov was not an

ordinary person, having served under Boris

Yeltsin as economic adviser; he was able to

fatten his pockets during the privatization

process that the Russian government had

implemented in the late 1980's. His major

investment of money derived from corruption,

in to the American real estate and construction

VAN CARLTON DETECTIVE AGENCY

markets after the American economic recession of 2008, made him even richer.

There were three security guards at the entrance of the Poplov residence and Rory Poplov was himself standing at the entrance of the door to his house. The security guards walked briskly towards Jennifer and Van Carlton and walked them to the entrance.

CHAPTER SEVEN

POPLOV

Rory Poplov greeted them and welcomed them in to his home.

VAN CARLTON DETECTIVE AGENCY

"What is it I can do for you lady and gentlemen?" he said with a thick Russian accent

"My name is Steve Van Carlton of the Van Carlton Detective Agency, I am a private detective hired to find a missing jewel, the Burgundy Diamond. It has been stolen from the Biltmore Hotel and we are investigating it."

"I have no problem helping you out. Why would I know anything about it?" Poplov said

Van Carlton responded "Your fingerprint was found on the glass case that held the Burgundy Diamond."

VAN CARLTON DETECTIVE AGENCY

"Ha. Ha. Ha." Poplov laughed "Look closer on the glass Mr. Van Carlton, I own the company that made the glass, Poplov Glass Industries. I inspect all important and expensive products that we create."

Van Carlton responded "Did you attend the exhibition at the Biltmore?"

"I did attend, you know I attended as do the press that printed an article with a picture of me in it." Poplov said

"Excuse me for asking Mr. Poplov. Where were you last night between 3am to 5am?" Van Carlton asked

VAN CARLTON DETECTIVE AGENCY

Poplov responded "I don't see how that concerns you. Look, I have told you what I know. You have to excuse me now as I have a meeting and guests I must attend to."

Poplov stood up and walked out the room, with three private bodyguards trailing behind him.

Jennifer and Van Carlton were shown to the door, they proceeded to the BMW 740il, and drove away. Poplov and his lawyer were watching this from their closed circuit security camera system that they were able to access from the apps on their Nokia smartphones.

VAN CARLTON
DETECTIVE AGENCY

"That is the last we shall be seeing of Mr. Van Carlton." Poplov's lawyer said

"I don't imagine that to be true, he seems like a wily character but a man that always finishes the job. Better to not take risks, have arrangements been for Amsterdam?" Poplov said

"They have." Poplov's lawyer said

"Good" said Poplov

The meeting with Poplov had made Van Carlton feel uneasy. Van Carlton felt there was something that Poplov was hiding. Van Carlton called Marin.

VAN CARLTON DETECTIVE AGENCY

"I want a trace placed on all communications going to and from the Poplov residence." Van Carlton said

Marin responded "That will take a week and I need to do the paperwork for seeing the judge."

"Cut the crap Marin. I need a trace now. We don't have a week. I think we have found the culprit. I am not sure though but my gut tells me it is him. I want a communications and physical trace." Van Carlton said

Marin said "Physical trace? That means bodies and time."

VAN CARLTON DETECTIVE AGENCY

"We don't have time. Call in the regulars, the number is in the top drawer in my desk. Oh and Marin, no more mistakes. This is our chance to really stamp our name." Van Carlton said

"Yes boss" Marin said

Poplov left his residence in a bulletproof Maybach, being trailed by two black Suburbans, his security detail. A white Toyota Corolla with two Van Carlton agents inside trailed them. Poplov arrived at a warehouse on the outskirts of town in a distressed area of run-down factories in Torrance.

VAN CARLTON DETECTIVE AGENCY

CHAPTER EIGHT

THE RAID

Gordon and Yang Wong, famous for their love of criminality and cyber-terrorism arrived at the warehouse.

"Thank you for coming gentlemen." said Poplov

"We would not miss this Poplov." Mark Gordon said

They entered the warehouse and there were elaborate decorations and tables set up. Scantily clad women were partying and dancing all over the place, champagne was flowing, and there were two wrestlers throwing

VAN CARLTON
DETECTIVE AGENCY

each around for their enjoyment. Poplov,

Gordon, Wong and his associates sat down.

Gordon said "We know you have the diamond

Poplov."

Poplov said "I may just have it. What is it worth

to you?"

Gordon and Wong, famous for their years of

cyber-terrorism and drug pushing, had made

themselves both rich and famous. They were

able to bully other gangsters using extortion as

their tool of choice and their drug sales

reached epic proportions.

VAN CARLTON
DETECTIVE AGENCY

Wong said "We will give you anything you need

Poplov. Guns, drugs, what can we give you?

We have spent our lives making our enemies

miserable. And we have also made our friends

rich and fat. But you, Poplov, have to work

with us."

Poplov said "I am working with the highest

payer. You know why I am in this business,

you can bid like the rest of our guests."

Poplov stood up and approached the podium.

This was not a sale. This was an auction and

the attendees were the largest international

criminals in the world. The international

VAN CARLTON
DETECTIVE AGENCY

criminals Gordon and Wong were waiting to bid and their years of drugs sales and harassment of others had paid off big time, as now they were in the big leagues.

"The price starts at three hundred million dollars. Who make the first bid?" Poplov said

The crowd fell silent. They looked amongst themselves and they were all wondering who would make the first move. To these criminals, whoever made the first move, would be the loser and a special silence overtook the crowd.

Just as the auction was going to start, the distance sound of a helicopter fast approaching

VAN CARLTON DETECTIVE AGENCY

was heard. Police car sirens blaring interrupted the sound of the helicopter and the criminals dispersed in awaiting limos. When the police arrived, all they found was an empty warehouse with an untouched catering table. As the investigation started and the officers began pointing fingers as to who was responsible for this mistake, Van Carlton arrived and parked. He walked pass the yellow lines that had cordoned off the warehouse and entered through the front entrance of the massive industrial building. Detective Montessori greeted him.

VAN CARLTON DETECTIVE AGENCY

"Been a long time Van Carlton. I thought you were dead." said Montessori

"Yeah you and the rest of L.A." Van Carlton replied

"Here on official business?" said Montessori

"I am not working my usual case of the missing scumbag. I am on the Burgundy Diamond case. Do you got any tips for me?" Van Carlton said

"Yeah. Start looking in Europe. That is where I would be if I had the Burgundy Diamond. I doubt there are any local criminals that would

VAN CARLTON DETECTIVE AGENCY

pay the high sum the thief is asking for." said Montessori

"Even still. I have reason to believe the thief is an important business man with roots in Los Angeles. Here is my card with my updated contact info on it. Do me a favor and call me if you hear anything. I will leave it up to LA's finest. See you soon Montessori." said Van Carlton walking off to his car.

"See you around Van Carlton." replied Montessori

Montessori's long time work partner Detective Raines walked up to Montessori.

VAN CARLTON DETECTIVE AGENCY

"Haven't seen that fellow in a long time. I thought he was dead." said Raines

"Yeah, you, me, and Los Angeles included. Says he is working on the Burgundy Diamond case now. A fellow like that must be making a lot of money working for these rich art owners and such." Montessori said

"Think he's on the take?" replied Raines

"No way. A person like that is as straight as whole wheat. You probably can't find a more honest cop. Let me know if you hear anything about the Burgundy Diamond case Raines." said Montessori

VAN CARLTON DETECTIVE AGENCY

CHAPTER NINE

GIVE IT A REST

Van Carlton needed a rest until some simple things were understood better. What was the relation of Poplov, Nardin and Kilroy to the robbery? Was the recent LAPD operation on the warehouse related to the theft or was there something else under this? Van Carlton needed to refresh his mind. He pulled in to the fitness center headquarters where he had been paying for workouts twice a month with famed fitness celebrity Tony Horton. This guy was famous for his P90X fitness tapes that had made so many people slim right from the

VAN CARLTON
DETECTIVE AGENCY

comforts of their house. But Van Carlton was

not at home, he was paying $1,000 an hour for

these lessons and every costly minute

counted. Ton y was waiting in the lobby to

greet him.

"How is it going bud? You ready to bring it?"
Tony Horton said

They high fived each other.

"Always." replied Van Carlton

"Good. Get changed. See you on the floor in

five." Tony said

VAN CARLTON DETECTIVE AGENCY

Van Carlton went through an hour of grueling calisthenics combined with yoga and isometric exercises, all the while thinking over the case.

There has to be a simple explanation as to the theft, Van Carlton thought to himself.

The session ended and Van Carlton showered, changed in to a chic Emanuel Ungaro suit and headed out for the night. He was thinking of the case all day and he needed a break. The last thing he wanted was to think about it more for the night. His car raced up Santa Monica Boulevard toward Sepulveda. He raced up Sepulveda Boulevard through the windy roads

VAN CARLTON DETECTIVE AGENCY

leading through the shaded canyons towards

the San Fernando Valley. He was invited for an

evening of dinner, drinks, and possibly

macabre at the mansion of a local debutante,

Selma Winston. Van Carlton had went through

a string of broken relationships and failed love

affairs, so he was not ready for commitment.

Many of the women that dated Van Carlton

would have admitted that he had never been

ready for commitment. So here was a chance

to get in to the "game" again, as he felt

confident after his grueling work-out session,

and was ready for the night's entertainment.

He arrived at the home of Selma Winston after

VAN CARLTON
DETECTIVE AGENCY

passing through the guard gated community

entrance, past the custom man-made lake

erected for the amusement of the

neighborhood's millionaires. A valet greeted

him, Van Carlton exited and walked toward the

front door, again to be greeted by the host, the

fabulous Selma Winston. Selma was an

actress, an activist, philanthropist, world

traveler, martial artist, and poet. She became

famous for her roles in a few Hollywood

produced action-adventures films. She quickly

faded in to the crowd of up and coming starlets

but was turned off by the industry. She felt

surrounded by "yes men" and overly ambitious

VAN CARLTON DETECTIVE AGENCY

people that would do anything for fifteen minutes of fame. If Selma wasn't holding a protest sign in her hand fighting for some obscure social cause, she was working in the community doing volunteer work at a soup kitchen. She cared about people and saw the ability to touch people's hearts as being more important than touching people's wallets. She was trusted and had friends of many different cultures and backgrounds. She prided herself on having the common touch despite having grown up in a third generation oil family. She was educated at Yale but also was very personable and that would draw people to her.

VAN CARLTON DETECTIVE AGENCY

She was not only a member of Greenpeace International, she used to proudly show the picture from the local newspaper's article from the time she was arrested at a sit-in against oil drilling in the arctic. Selma had met Van Carlton at a wedding many years ago and they had been friends since.

"Welcome old friend." said Selma

"Oh, I am not that old yet. Still young I suppose." Van Carlton said

"You look handsome." said Selma

VAN CARLTON DETECTIVE AGENCY

"Mersi. Mademoiselle. You look beautiful tonight as always. Now won't you offer a gentleman a drink?" Van Carlton said

"Certainly. Follow me." Selma said while grinning excitedly

Van Carlton followed her inside to the main bar in the house, a very large mahogany bar stretching alongside the room, approximately ten meters long. The bar had brass columns with a mirror behind the bartender, with the words "Audemus Jura Nostra Defendere" etched in to it. Van Carlton mind started racing

VAN CARLTON DETECTIVE AGENCY

and thinking, attempting to translate this simple

Latin statement.

"Ah. Audemus Jura Nostra Defendere. Latin for

we dare defend our rights. Also on Alabama's

state flag. Interesting." Van Carlton said

"Yes. Thank you. Although I really can't claim

credit for it, it was on the mirror when I

purchased the house in 2005. But thank you.

So what made you come out and play tonight?

I mean you are always working and never have

time to spend with us boring folks." said Selma

"I was working today. I have a new case. The

Burgundy Diamond was stolen recently and

VAN CARLTON DETECTIVE AGENCY

business has never been better. But I did miss you and I would not miss your soirée, you know that." Van Carlton said

"The Burgundy Diamond? Oh my, I saw something about it in the news. What is that worth these days?" Selma said

"Two hundred maybe three hundred million dollars. There has never been a price really set on it. If you ask me, it is priceless." Van Carlton replied

The rest of the night passed in apparent gaiety and happiness was found everywhere, as the guests ate the finest sushi catered by Katsuya

VAN CARLTON
DETECTIVE AGENCY

and drank the most expensive bottles of liquor

they could muster in their drunken fervor. The

guests were leaving and it was getting late, but

Van Carlton was intercepted by Selma before

he could leave out the front door.

"Leaving so soon?" Selma said

"What did you have in mind?" Van Carlton

replied

"You look tired. Why don't you spend the night

and keep a gal company." Selma said

"I don't see why not." Van Carlton replied

VAN CARLTON DETECTIVE AGENCY

The guests were escorted out by the staff and Van Carlton followed Selma upstairs....

CHAPTER TEN

THE FIND

The next day arrived quickly and Van Carlton was tired. He did not stop to rest though and decided to keep going further. Maybe a little too far this time. He decided to enter the Poplov mansion covertly. He drove outside the estate and parked at a distance of 200 meters from the front gate. He sat in the car, listening on his digital voice receiver to phone calls that he had intercepted in the past few days. One of the telephone messages had

VAN CARLTON DETECTIVE AGENCY

to be the clue. He listened to the first few messages and luckily found what he was looking for. It was a message from Wong, one of the buyers at the raided auction Poplov was hosting. Apparently Wong was frustrated from waiting for the diamond and thought it would be easier to get rid of Poplov quietly and take the Burgundy Diamond. So Poplov did have the diamond, Van Carlton thought to himself. Now that Van Carlton knew, he could take the evidence to the police and the thought of the bureaucracy involved made his re-consider. He could just walk in and confront Van Carlton with the evidence and with options for returning. More likely than not, Van Carlton would be shot dead before Poplov would be giving back the Burgundy Diamond. He had to leave or do what he had come here to do, that was see Poplov. Either he would get a welcome reception or lead, but sitting in the car any further was making him feel uneasy.

He jumped the nearest wall, no small feat as it was approximately 8 feet tall. From the wall, he jumped on to a tree and landed safely on the soft grass lawn. He quickly hid behind the tree and saw two private security guards outside the French doors leading in to the living room. There was a mid-sized

VAN CARLTON
DETECTIVE AGENCY

designer pool between the house and the tree.
Van Carlton picked up a rock and threw it in
the pool, creating a diversion. One of the
guards walked towards the pool and stopped,
looking at the tree. The guard walked around
the pool and towards the tree. Van Carlton had
to think quickly. He had to fight his way in or
make up some nonsensical story on why he
was standing in Poplov's yard.

He was tired of mucking around and the entire
case was on his nerves. As the guard walked
up, Van Carlton jumped out.

VAN CARLTON
DETECTIVE AGENCY

"Hi. Sorry to startle you guy. I am with Publishers Clearing House. I am here to award the prize to a Mr. Poplov." Van Carlton said

The guard pulled out his gun and pointed it at Van Carlton. The second guard ran up and drew his pistol as well.

"Very funny tough guy. You're trespassing and you are going to have to leave now." The second guard said

"Am I in some kind of trouble?" Van Carlton said

VAN CARLTON DETECTIVE AGENCY

The first security guard said "Who let you in? You are not authorized to be here. We must escort you out."

"Okay, you got me. I lied. I am here because there are people that are going to attack Poplov." Van Carlton said

The second security guard said "People? What people? When?"

"I need to speak with Poplov!" Van Carlton said

The guards escorted Van Carlton in to the house, towards Poplov's private office. Poplov was waiting for them, only he had two bullets shot in his chest and he was lying face down

VAN CARLTON DETECTIVE AGENCY

on his $100,000 mahogany desk. As soon as they entered, each guard on either side of Van Carlton were lit up with short-burst shots and collapsed. Van Carlton was stunned, but he managed to pull out his revolver and ran towards the stairs. Shots rained at him and he hid behind a marble column in the hallway.

A voice rang out from behind the stairs "There is no use. The diamond is not here."

"Who the hell are you? Why did you kill Poplov?" Van Carlton said

The voice from behind the stairs said "We are giving you one chance to walk out that door.

VAN CARLTON
DETECTIVE AGENCY

Only one chance. If you leave quietly, you will live. If not, you will be dead before you fire a single shot."

"I am looking for the Burgundy Diamond. Return it and I will protect you from arrest." Van Carlton replied

Van Carlton waited 20 seconds but no answer. He picked up a small piece of mirror that was broken on the floor. He held it out with his right arm to look at the shooters. The mirror was shot out of his hand.

"Damn it! I am tired of playing with you assholes!" Van Carlton said

VAN CARLTON DETECTIVE AGENCY

Van Carlton looked out to the column adjacent to him and took off his jacket. He threw his jacket in the air towards the column, immediately drawing fire from two gunners, and he stepped out firing on both gunners. He hit the first one in the temple, immediately killing him. The second one he wounded, enough to approach him for information. As the second gunner was laying in agony, squirming and talking nonsense, Van Carlton stood over him with his gun pointed at him.

"Now, I am giving you one chance to speak up. Only one chance. Who stole the Burgundy Diamond?" Van Carlton said

VAN CARLTON DETECTIVE AGENCY

"Wong. He took the Burgundy Diamond and killed Poplov. You won't find him. He is gone, boarding his jet. Please don't kill me..." The second gunner said

Van Carlton almost felt sorry for him, decided to leave the scene and head off Wong before he fled the country. He took off his in his car towards LAX as that was his best guess to where Wong would be. As one of the busiest airports in the world, finding Wong would not be east. It would be like finding a needle in a haystack. The airport was packed as usual, wave after wave of cars entering and leaving, creating a perpetual traffic jam. He arrived at

VAN CARLTON DETECTIVE AGENCY

the LAPD substation in LAX and met with the Precinct Commander, showed him a picture of Wong. Immediately police cars scrambled and there was the feeling of excitement among these officers. A two hour search yielded no results. Van Carlton was growing weary and gave up his search at LAX. He drove to Santa Monica airport and after supplying the appropriate credentials and a few bribes like tickets to a Celine Dion concert, he was able to gather that Wong had left the country in a private jet, destination France. This was getting more interesting by the minute. Why France? Nardin had his roots in France and

VAN CARLTON DETECTIVE AGENCY

had his main offices there. Was Nardin involved? Nardin was an original suspect that Van Carlton perceived to have had some involvement in this robbery. But maybe it was that Nardin had no hand in the theft but was now involved. This was a possibility that Van Carlton did not want to rule out. Van Carlton did not have many choices, so he made the best one he could. He purchased a round trip flight with Air France to Paris. Van Carlton boarded the flight a few hours later and after a 10 hour flight, arrived at the city he had spent much time in his youth with his parents, Paris. The Seine River flowing through the city made

VAN CARLTON DETECTIVE AGENCY

this place a favorite for him. His trips to the Louvre Museum to see the Mona Lisa, ancient artifacts, and cultural landmarks, broadened Van Carlton's artistic sensibilities. But he was not here on vacation, he was here to catch a thief. His first visit would be to Nardin.

CHAPTER ELEVEN

THE RUNNER

Van Carlton arrived outside Nardin Tech International offices and met with a press representative of the company named Peter Morris. Morris spoke English fluently and had arranged a meeting for him. Nardin Tech International's building was gargantuan, a

VAN CARLTON DETECTIVE AGENCY

behemoth among its neighbors. As a tech

innovator, they had created the first wearable

instant translation device that had now been

widely adopted by diplomats of the United

Nations. This gadget not only made Mr. Nardin

rich, it made him very famous. His philanthropy

was felt on five continents. Van Carlton was

eager to question Nardin, although this was not

an official meeting and Van Carlton had no

jurisdiction in France. He was here on a fact

finding mission and if he thought that Nardin

was involved and had the evidence to back up

the claim, Van Carlton had contacts in the

Paris police forces that he could get help from.

VAN CARLTON DETECTIVE AGENCY

Van Carlton was sitting outside Nardin's office, when he received an anonymous phone call.

"The Burgundy Diamond is going to be sold at an auction in Amsterdam in two days. At the Krasnapolsky Hotel, 2pm...." The mysterious voice said

The phone was hung up.

Nardin walked out of his office, welcomed Van Carlton and lead him in to his artistically decorated office. Renaissance paintings and tapestries adorned Nardin's spatial office overlooking the beauty of Paris. This was a huge change from the LA offices.

VAN CARLTON
DETECTIVE AGENCY

"How can I help you, Mr. Van Carlton?" Nardin

said

"Thank you for seeing me on such short notice.

Our first meeting ended so abruptly that I did

not have a chance to talk with you thoroughly."

Van Carlton said

"I told you at our first meeting that I have no

information on the theft. Why are you in

France?" Nardin replied

"I followed the person believed to have stolen

it, a fellow named Wong, to Paris. This meeting

is informal really. I wanted your help that is all.

VAN CARLTON
DETECTIVE AGENCY

Have you learned any new information about the Burgundy Diamond?" Van Carlton said

"I unfortunately have no information on the Burgundy Diamond as I said earlier. Moreover, I am surprised it is in France. I would think it would have been sold already. If I receive any information, I will get it to you. Please give me your card Mr. Van Carlton." Nardin replied

Van Carlton gave Nardin his business card, thanked him for the meeting, and left with Morris to the front, entering a company car that drove him back to the hotel George V. George

VAN CARLTON DETECTIVE AGENCY

V was an internationally famous hotel. Its lobby was filled with the jet-set crowd of super-millionaires and diplomats. Wives of rich oil sheikhs wearing the most extravagant diamond jewelry were sipping tea and talking about their shopping sprees. Van Carlton just wanted to get some rest so he avoided the scene and walked up the stairs to his room. Roughly five minutes after entering his room and getting comfortable, a note was slipped under the door. Peculiar, Van Carlton thought, as no one knew he was here other than his assistants.

VAN CARLTON DETECTIVE AGENCY

Van Carlton proceeded to open the note and it read:

Meet me at Fouquet's at 8pm sharp, if you want to know about the diamond.

Van Carlton had been to Fouquet's on a few special occasions. Known as a haunt for aristocrats of French society, he was more than happy to knock back a few spirits and shoot the proverbial _merde'_.

Van Carlton arrived 15 minutes early, but was greeted and given a table unusually fast. A middle-aged man, approximately 45, approached Van Carlton and sat down.

VAN CARLTON
DETECTIVE AGENCY

"I did not think you would show up." The man said

"I never miss an invitation to dinner, especially when the person is paying for me. So now I am here. And you are?" Van Carlton replied

"My name is Bernard. Yes, I called you about the diamond auction. I am an accountant. I used to work for Nardin. I was fired less than a few days ago when I brought to his attention a large number of suspicious transactions. He knew that I found out about his secret dealings, so he fired me. I still have my sources inside. People that are close to Nardin. This is payback for me. I will tell you what I know. The diamond will be sold in two days time. At the Krasnapolsky Hotel. A suite has been rented and less than 5 buyers have been invited. This is all I know."

"Why should I trust this information. I don't know who you are. You could be giving me wrong information. Why should I trust you?" Van Carlton said

"Because I am the only hope you got" Bernard said

VAN CARLTON DETECTIVE AGENCY

CHAPTER TWELVE

THE DAM

Van Carlton arrived in Schipol Airport by way of Thalys high speed train from Paris-Noord station in France. The train ride lasted three and a half hours with the train travelling at speeds up to 330 kilometers per hour. From Schipol, Van Carlton took the city train arriving at Amsterdam Centraal Station, from which he took a taxi for ten euros to Dam Square. Dam Square was among the oldest parts of the city, with buildings dating back to the 1600's. In its beautiful square was situated many Amsterdam landmarks. Surrounding Dam

VAN CARLTON DETECTIVE AGENCY

Square was the department store De Bijenkorf, the Krasnapolsky Hotel started by Wilhelm Krasnapolsky in the 1700's, and the Amsterdam Royal Palace from which Queen Beatrix had ruled for many decades. Van Carlton's ancestors had immigrated from the Netherlands to the United States in the early 1900's and his grandparents would speak Dutch to him as a boy. He was a few minutes early as usual and decided to walk in the Krasnapolsky Hotel. He walked past the Krasnapolsky's most famous room, the Winter Garden, a giant ballroom situated between two wings of the hotel. He had informed his friend

VAN CARLTON DETECTIVE AGENCY

in the Dutch police, Joost De Groot, that he might need his help and Joost being the friendly person he was, had happily agreed. In an instant the entire focus shifted! Van Carlton just saw Nardin walking in the hallway! Van Carlton followed him to the suites and entered the stairway at a distance. He followed Nardin up to the 2nd floor where there were two guards outside its entrance. Nardin entered the suite and the door closed behind him. Van Carlton was here to find information and pass it on. He was not here to crash the party. But being the tough guy he was, he was going in head first. He walked up to the two bodyguards and pulled out his wallet as if to show something in it, thereby drawing the attention to this wallet. He pulled out a piece of paper with scribbling on it and dropped it in front of the hands of one of the guards, as that guard lowered his gaze, Van Carlton knocked him out with a swift and well executed uppercut. The other guard reached for the gun in his waist belt but was stopped by Van Carlton's elbow to the guard's face. Van Carlton grabbed the guard in a front headlock choke, till the guard passed out. Both guards were passed out and Van Carlton opened the door swiftly. There was no one there. It was a hallway with three doors. Van

VAN CARLTON DETECTIVE AGENCY

Carlton entered the door adjacent to the entrance. Van Carlton walked in and the scene looked like a proper auction with an illegitimate object for sale, the Burgundy Diamond. Gordon, Wong aka The Fox, Nardin, Kilroy, and a man later found to be named Zeno, were there. The auction stopped and the room fell silent with Van Carlton's appearance.

Gordon and Wong pulled out pistols, pointing them at Van Carlton.

"Gentlemen please, put those away. I have alerted the Dutch police, they will be here in less than 5 minutes." Van Carlton said

VAN CARLTON DETECTIVE AGENCY

"Nardin good to see you here. I always knew you had no part in this." Van Carlton said sarcastically

"Oh shut up idiot. If it wasn't for your meddling this auction would have been done already." Nardin replied frustrated

"I say you all let me kill him and dump his body in the Amstel River." Zeno said

Kilroy pulled out a pistol, pointed it at Wong, Zeno, Gordon and said "No leave him alone. Let us finish the auction."

Gordon and Wong pointed their pistols at Kilroy and said "He alerted the police, there is no

112

VAN CARLTON DETECTIVE AGENCY

more auction, we are leaving but not without the diamond."

"I think what we have here boys is called a Mexican Standoff. And you know how this turns out. " Kilroy said

Gordon fired at Kilroy but missed, hitting and breaking the window behind him. Kilroy fired back with one bullet instantly hitting Gordon in the temple, killing him. Wong fired back and hit Kilroy in the shoulder, dropping him to the floor. Kilroy fired back from the floor killing Wong. Nardin fled but was tackled by Van Carlton and punched on the floor in to submission. Zeno

VAN CARLTON DETECTIVE AGENCY

had stayed silent and was for the first time shocked that this auction had turned from a friendly sale in to a kill zone. He looked at the Burgundy Diamond, pointed his gun at Van Carlton and said "It looks like you are the only one left. Say goodbye to your precious diamond, because it is the last time you are going to ever see it."

As Zeno cocked the hammer of his revolver, Joost De Groot entered the front door, pistol drawn and unloaded one bullet in to Zeno's abdomen. Zeno immediately fell unconscious. Dutch police were swarming the scene in minutes. Zeno, Kilroy, and Nardin were

VAN CARLTON DETECTIVE AGENCY

arrested. Gordon and Wong were attended to

by the coroner. All the thoughts of his journey

were swirling through his head and Van

Carlton started to re-think about the evolution

of the case. It was Poplov that had stolen the

Burgundy Diamond. His henchmen bribed and

threatened the highly underpaid security

guards protecting the Burgundy Diamond,

essentially walking out with the precious jewel

without so much as an alarm sounding. Gordon

and Wong were unable to purchase the

Burgundy Diamond at the first auction hosted

by Poplov, which was raided by police. They

killed Poplov at his home, stole the Burgundy

VAN CARLTON DETECTIVE AGENCY

Diamond and fled to Paris in hiding. The Fox was Wong, and he showed his cleverness by stealing the diamond from Poplov. But the second auction was hosted by Nardin on behalf of Wong, this much he later confessed to, as he was their contact and partners in Europe. The Burgundy Diamond had been recovered and returned to its rightful owner Mark Jostler, Van Carlton only had to spend a few days in the hospital, and he was able to enjoy a mandatory one month leave of absence in beautiful Amsterdam. What started as a journey in sunny Los Angeles ended in canal-filled Amsterdam.

VAN CARLTON DETECTIVE AGENCY

Short Story Review

1. How would you have ended the story differently?

2. Was Van Carlton the typical good guy? What is it about his character that made him unique?

3. The three suspects, Nardin, Kilroy, and Poplov, what was it about their characters that you liked or disliked?

4. If you could add a character to this story, who would they be? What would their qualities be and how would they change the outcome of the story?

VAN CARLTON DETECTIVE AGENCY

INDEX

VAN CARLTON
DETECTIVE AGENCY

MIKAZUKI PUBLISHING HOUSE TITLES
Stories of a Street Performer (Pop Haydn)
Swords & Sails: Legacy of the Red Lion (David McAvoy)
California's Next Century 2.0: Economic Renaissance (Evans)
Political Advertising Manual
Learning Magic
25 Principles of Martial Arts
Magic as Science & Religion
The Bribe Vibe
World War Water
Small Arms & Deep Pockets
Arctic Black Gold
Find the Ideal Husband
John Locke's 2nd Treatise on Civil Government (John Locke)
The History of Acid Tripping (Eric Hurtado)
I Dream In Haiku (German Sanchez)
Mikazuki Political Science Manual
Tokiwa; A Japanese Love Story (Onoto Watana)
The Card Party; Theater Play (JR Planche)
The Markinson Building

VAN CARLTON
DETECTIVE AGENCY

Hagakure; The Book of Hidden Leaves (Hiroki Shima)
MMA Coloring Book
DIY Comic Book
Freakshow Los Angeles (Carl Crew)
Karate 360
Coming to America Handbook (Terry Allen Dodson)
The Medium Writer (Terry Allen Dodson)
Mikazuki Jujitsu Manual
Self-Examination Diary: Good and Bad Deeds Log
Master Password Organizer Handbook
George Washington's Farewell Address (George Washington)
Customer Profile Organizer
United Nations Charter
DIY Comic Book Part II
Storyboard Book: Make Your Movie Series
Basketball Team Play Design Book
Football Play Design Book
T-Shirt Design Book
Rappers Rhyme Book: Lyricists Notebook
Japan History Coloring Book

VAN CARLTON
DETECTIVE AGENCY

Magicians Coloring Book
The Adventures of Sherlock Holmes
Words of King Darius
The Art of War
The Book of Five Rings
Tao Te Ching
Captain Bligh's Voyage
Beginner's Magician Manual
The Man that Made the English Language
The Arrival of Palloncino
The Irish Republican Army Manual of Guerrilla Warfare
Living the Pirate Code
Quotes Gone Wild
The Art of Western Boxing
Shogun X the Last Immortal: Scrolls of Partan Village
Tales from the Darkside of the Laundry (Kate Van Gilder Hunt)

VAN CARLTON
DETECTIVE AGENCY

MIKAZUKI PUBLISHING HOUSE BELIEVES IN:

- **Education is the Key to Happiness**

- **Stopping Deforestation (Plant Trees)**

- **Promoting Literacy**

- **Supporting Independent Bookstores**

- **Protecting Higher Education**

www.MikazukiPublishingHouse.com

How you can get involved:

Attend Book Signings

Shop at Independent Bookstores

Attend Book Fairs

Recycle regularly

Attend Libraries

VAN CARLTON
DETECTIVE AGENCY

NOTES

VAN CARLTON
DETECTIVE AGENCY

NOTES

VAN CARLTON DETECTIVE AGENCY

NOTES

VAN CARLTON
DETECTIVE AGENCY

NOTES

VAN CARLTON
DETECTIVE AGENCY

NOTES

VAN CARLTON
DETECTIVE AGENCY

NOTES

VAN CARLTON
DETECTIVE AGENCY

NOTES

VAN CARLTON
DETECTIVE AGENCY

NOTES

www.ingramcontent.com/pod-product-compliance
Lightning Source LLC
Chambersburg PA
CBHW021116130626
46554CB00002B/724

* 9 7 8 0 9 9 1 0 2 8 5 0 4 *